Military Animals

SUPPLY TRANSPORT ANIMALS

by Debbie Vilardi

abdobooks.com

Published by Pop!, a division of ABDO, PO Box 398166, Minneapolis, Minnesota 55289. Copyright ©2022 by Abdo Consulting Group, Inc. International copyrights reserved in all countries. No part of this book may be reproduced in any form without written permission from the publisher. DiscoverRoo™ is a trademark and logo of Pop!.

Printed in the United States of America, North Mankato, Minnesota.

102021
012022

THIS BOOK CONTAINS RECYCLED MATERIALS

Cover Photo: U.S. Marine Corps
Interior Photos: Shutterstock Images, 1; Defense Visual Information Distribution Service, 5, 7, 9, 17, 19, 21, 22, 23; US Army, 6; North Wind Picture Archives, 11, 12; AP Images, 13, 14; iStockphoto, 16; Uriel Sinai/Getty Images News/Getty Images, 25; ITAR-TASS News Agency/Alamy, 26, 27; Jigme Dorje Xinhua News Agency/Newscom, 29

Editor: Charly Haley
Series Designer: Laura Graphenteen

Library of Congress Control Number: 2020948917
Publisher's Cataloging-in-Publication Data
Names: Vilardi, Debbie, author.
Title: Supply transport animals / by Debbie Vilardi
Description: Minneapolis, Minnesota : Pop!, 2022 | Series: Military animals | Includes online resources and index.
Identifiers: ISBN 9781532169984 (lib. bdg.) | ISBN 9781644945933 (pbk.) | ISBN 9781098240912 (ebook)
Subjects: LCSH: Animals--Juvenile literature. | Working animals--Juvenile literature. | Transport service--Juvenile literature. | Armed Forces--Juvenile literature.
Classification: DDC 355.424--dc23

Pop open this book and you'll find QR codes loaded with information, so you can learn even more!

Scan this code* and others like it while you read, or visit the website below to make this book pop!

popbooksonline.com/supply-transport

*Scanning QR codes requires a web-enabled smart device with a QR code reader app and a camera.

TABLE OF CONTENTS

CHAPTER 1
Supply Mules 4

CHAPTER 2
A History of Service 10

CHAPTER 3
Why Animals? .18

CHAPTER 4
Around the World 24

Making Connections 30
Glossary 31
Index 32
Online Resources 32

CHAPTER 1

SUPPLY MULES

Soldiers climbed high on a rough path.

Each of them led a mule. The mules carried packs up the steep, narrow trail.

Military pack mules may carry food,

WATCH A VIDEO HERE!

Mules can help transport supplies over rough land.

water, and tents. They may also carry guns and bullets, first aid kits, and animal care items.

Military mules sometimes carry weapons, such as grenade launchers.

The soldiers were at a training camp in California. They were preparing for **deployment** to Afghanistan.

They learned to care for the animals.

The soldiers also learned how to pack and lead mules. Mules were important because they would carry supplies that soldiers needed.

Soldiers are friendly with the animals they care for.

Mules have carried soldiers and supplies for a long time. But they are not the only animals to do this. Other **transport** animals include elephants, horses, and camels. Donkeys, llamas, reindeer, and yaks sometimes help move supplies too.

DID YOU KNOW? The US military built a robotic mule between 2010 and 2015. It could carry 400 pounds (180 kg). But it was too loud to use. Enemies might have heard it.

Military horses don't just carry supplies. Sometimes they carry people too.

CHAPTER 2

A HISTORY OF SERVICE

Pack animals have been used by militaries since the beginning of **civilization**. War horses pulled **chariots** in the Middle East a long time ago. The chariots carried soldiers into battle until about 850 BCE.

LEARN MORE HERE!

Each chariot usually carried two people into battle.

Asian elephants were first used in war approximately 3,000 years ago. These animals are large and strong.

Militaries in Burma used elephants to carry supplies in the 1880s.

An elephant helps load supplies into an airplane at a US Air Force base in India in 1945.

They can walk through floods. Some militaries used elephants to move logs for construction, such as building roads and bridges. A small army in the country Burma still uses war elephants today.

Finland's army used sled dogs in 1940.

Alaskan sled dogs pulled **cargo** for the US Army between 1901 and 1905.

France used Alaskan sled dogs during

World War I (1914–1918). Americans used them in World War II (1939–1945). Horses and mules were commonly used during these wars too. All of these animals are still supply **transport** animals today. But the US Army no longer keeps sled dogs.

DID YOU KNOW? The US military used camels as transport animals in the 1850s. But when the Civil War (1861–1865) started, the military stopped using camels. It didn't have enough money to care for them.

TIMELINE

1,100 BCE
Elephants are first used for military transport.

850 BCE
After many years, militaries stop using horses to pull chariots during battle, though they keep using horses for other jobs.

1980s
The United States brings mules to Afghanistan to help the Afghans defeat the Soviets. The mules easily carry weapons in the mountains.

1941
Reindeer join the Soviet Union's military. In the cold and snow, reindeer prove to be better for supply transport than horses and vehicles.

2008
The US Marine Corps starts the Animal Packers Course to teach military members how to work with pack animals.

CHAPTER 3

WHY ANIMALS?

Jeeps, trucks, planes, and boats move military supplies. But it's harder for enemies to see and hear **transport** animals. These animals can also go where vehicles can't.

COMPLETE AN ACTIVITY HERE!

Mules travel on paths that are narrow and steep. They climb to places in mountains where helicopters cannot fly. A donkey may stop if it senses danger. No supply truck can do that.

Soldiers may lead several pack mules together.

LEARNING TO WORK WITH ANIMALS

The soldiers who work with supply transport animals also need training. Many of them do not know much about animals at the beginning. Some start by learning the difference between a mule and a horse. Mules are part horse and part donkey. They are usually smaller than horses. But both animals are strong enough to carry heavy loads. After 16 days of training, the soldiers know how to pack and lead animals.

Soldiers train supply transport animals. Animals learn to follow soldiers. They must trust soldiers.

A soldier calls to the animal to come to her. If the animal comes, it gets a treat as a reward. Then the soldier packs the animal.

A US Marine leads a pack mule with a rope during training.

She attaches a rope to it. The soldier uses

the rope to lead the animal on the trail.

A soldier brushes his pack mule before loading the animal with supplies.

Animals must learn to carry heavy loads. Trainers use light loads first. They start with a single blanket. Slowly they add more weight. Soon the animals have saddles with full packs.

DID YOU KNOW? The US military has veterinarians to care for its animals.

PACK MULE EQUIPMENT

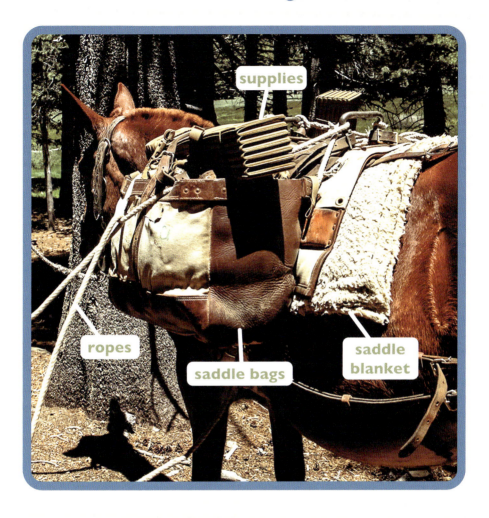

Pack mules do not only carry equipment for soldiers. They are also in charge of their own equipment too. Saddle bags and blankets help mules carry supplies comfortably. Soldiers use ropes to lead and tie up the mules.

CHAPTER 4

AROUND THE WORLD

Militaries around the world use **pack animals**. Different animals work well in different types of **terrain**.

In some places animals are being replaced by technology. The Israeli

LEARN MORE HERE!

military used to have llamas. A llama can carry 70 pounds (32 kg) of gear. It can walk on rough ground. But the Israeli military replaced them with robots in 2017.

Llamas carried weapons and other gear for Israeli soldiers.

Russian soldiers learn how to handle reindeer sleds during training.

Reindeer live in the snowy north.

They can carry heavy loads or pull sleds.

A reindeer sled can easily cross ice.

Several northern militaries have used reindeer. Russian soldiers still use them. They trained with reindeer and sled dogs in 2016 and 2017.

Sled dogs help militaries in snowy areas.

Yaks also do well in snow. They are like large, woolly cows. They live high in the mountains around China. The Chinese military uses them to carry soldiers and supplies.

Supply **transport** animals are military helpers. They carry and pull heavy loads. This makes a soldier's work easier.

There is an Animals in War Memorial in London, England. It includes bronze statues of pack mules.

Yaks can breathe easily in the high mountains. This helps them carry supplies.

MAKING CONNECTIONS

TEXT-TO-SELF

How do you transport things? Do you put items in a backpack? What would it be like if you used an animal to transport stuff?

TEXT-TO-TEXT

Have you read other books about military animals? How were the animals in those books similar to or different from the ones in this book?

TEXT-TO-WORLD

Militaries around the world use transport animals. What do you think militaries would be like if they couldn't use any animals?

GLOSSARY

cargo — items loaded for transport.

chariot — a cart pulled by animals that people can ride in.

civilization — the places and ways of life developed by humans.

deployment — a assignment that involves being sent or placed somewhere, usually for military work.

pack animal — an animal used for carrying cargo.

terrain — the physical features of a place.

transport — to move something from one place to another.

INDEX

camels, 8, 15

donkeys, 8, 19, 20

elephants, 8, 12–13, 16

horses, 8, 10, 15, 16–17, 20

llamas, 8, 25

mules, 4, 7–8, 15, 17, 19, 20, 23, 28

reindeer, 8, 17, 26–27

soldiers, 4, 6–8, 10, 20–21, 23, 27–28

yaks, 8, 28

ONLINE RESOURCES
popbooksonline.com

Scan this code* and others like it while you read, or visit the website below to make this book pop!

popbooksonline.com/supply-transport

*Scanning QR codes requires a web-enabled smart device with a QR code reader app and a camera.